Shomrei Torah Synagogue
Education Center
7353 Valley Circle Blvd
West Hills, California 91304

Sarah

Written by Illana Katz

Edited and Epilogue by Morris Paulson, Ph.D.

Preface by Dr. Elijah J. Schochet

Illustrations by Terry Wilson

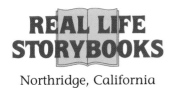

REAL LIFE
STORYBOOKS

Northridge, California

"Acts of goodness and kindness bestow immortality."

Our special thanks to Doctor Alan D. Rosenthal...

Other storybooks published by REAL LIFE STORYBOOKS include:

Joey and Sam
Show Me Where It Hurts
Uncle Jimmy

Published by

REAL LIFE STORYBOOKS
8370 Kentland Avenue
West Hills CA 91304

First Edition
Copyright © 1994

Library of Congress Cataloging-in-Publication Data

Katz, Illana, 1946–
Sarah/written by Illana Katz; illustrations by Terry Wilson; preface by Elijah J. Schochet;
prologue by Illana Katz; epilogue by Morris J. Paulson. --1st ed. p.   cm.

Summary: Sarah is shocked and saddened when Uncle Jack hurts her and touches her in private places,
and with the help of Doctor Good she finds the strength to tell.

Hardcover—ISBN # 1-882388-07-0: $16.95
Softcover—ISBN # 1-882388-08-9: $9.95

[1. Child molesting–Fiction.   2. Uncles–Fiction.]
I. Wilson, Terry, ill. II. Title.

PZ7.K15744Sar   1993
[E] – dc20

93-26429
CIP AC

This storybook may be purchased from the publisher, but try your local bookstore first.

Dedicated To Children Everywhere.

To Janice

Shield of Innocence

Do not forsake me with blind eyes and deaf ears,

Nor abandon me by turning away,

Leaving me unprotected.

But shield me,

Enriching my soul within your safe haven,

Arming me with all the

Wisdom,

Love,

Encouragement,

And

Understanding,

Only you can provide.

For I did not ask to be placed in your care,

But was invited.

Illana Katz

PREFACE

When it comes to today's moral and ethical standards, it seems that there is not much our world still agrees upon. There is, however, one exception, humanity's sanction against incest.

The subject of incest is our number one taboo! The very thought of children being abused by their own kin has led to a "see no evil, hear no evil, speak no evil" response. We don't want to believe the unbelievable, and so we remain blind to the evidence. Children's fears are discounted, children's tears are disregarded, children's anxieties are dismissed and when they persist...resented. "What is the matter with you? Why do you keep acting up? What in heaven's name are you so frightened for? Act your age. Be nice to Uncle Jack."

The result is trauma heaped upon trauma. The child who has been violated is made to feel as a violator of family harmony. The victim is the one being blamed. What the child tries so painfully to articulate remains unheard, and so humiliation and guilt intensify.

With remarkable lucidity and deep sensitivity, Illana Katz has crafted a welcome and long-overdue literary response to the challenge of incest. Though she has presented her storybook gently and even pleasantly, she firmly guides us to honestly confront this number one taboo and enables us to both articulate and to hear these all too often unspoken and unheard fears and guilts. Illana Katz's is "a book for all ages," figuratively and literally, helping us to confront what is possibly the universally acknowledged number one horror of all ages.

Dr. Elijah J. Schochet
Adjunct Professor of Rabbinics
University of Judaism
Los Angeles, California

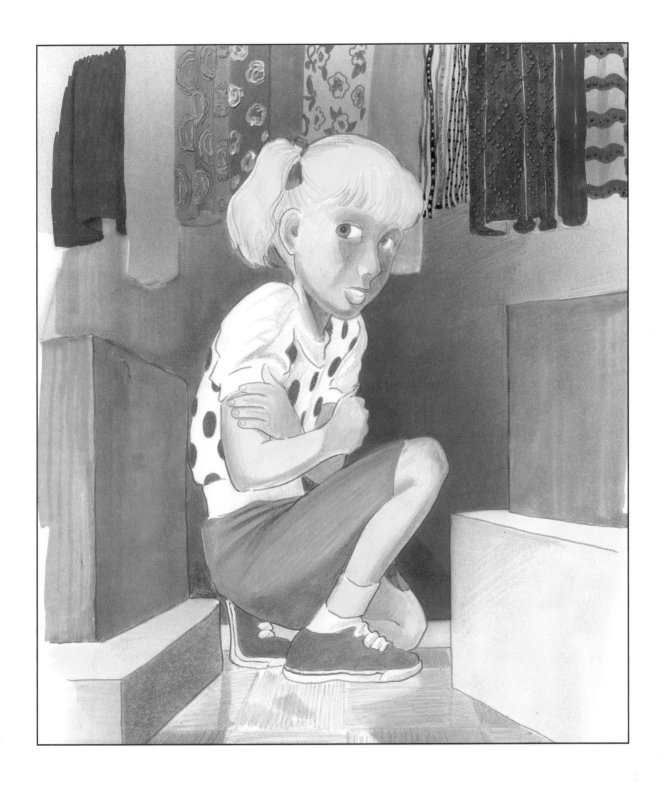

Sarah sat very still on her closet floor. It was dark and stuffy. She was hiding. The bottom of her dresses tickled her head as she strained to listen to the world outside her closet.

"I know you're here, Sarah," sang the soft voice of her uncle.
"I want to see you. I promise I won't hurt you."

Sarah did not move. She tried not to breathe.
Even at eight years old she knew truth from lie,
and her uncle told lies. He told lies to her,
and he told lies to her mother and father.
Sarah wished he had never come to live with them.

"Dear Sarah," teased her uncle as he pulled open the closet
door. "You know how I love to be with you,
and I know you love to be with me, too."

That was not true.
Because of Uncle Jack, Sarah felt different from other children.
Because of him she felt dirty.
Because of him she had secrets down deep inside,
secrets she was afraid to tell anyone,
secrets she was sure nobody would believe.
Sarah closed her eyes.
She kneeled down and waited for him to touch her in her
private places like he always did at times like these.
Sarah knew this was wrong. But what could she do?
He was a grownup and she was only eight years old.

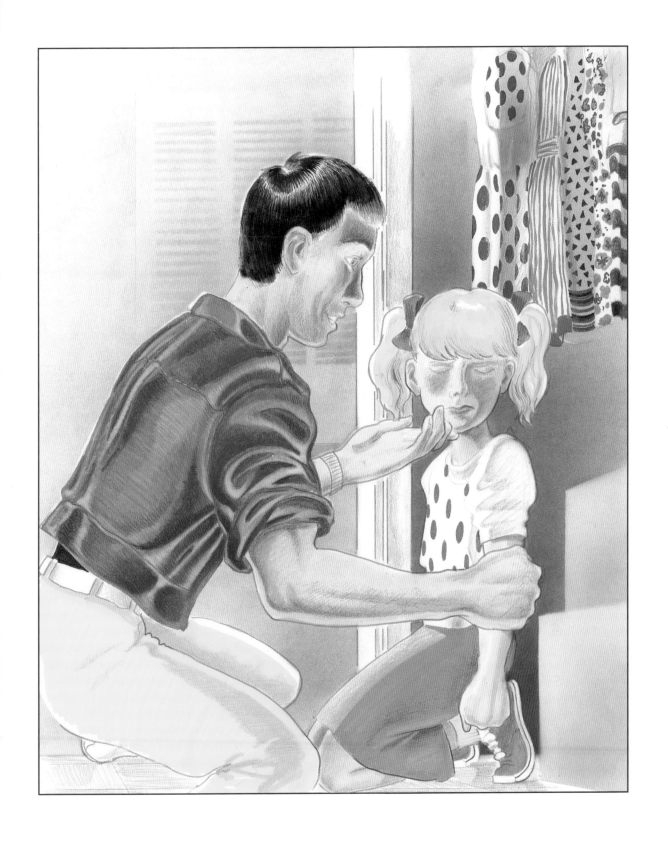

"Oh please," she prayed to herself, "Make him go away."

As if by magic her bedroom door suddenly opened and in stepped her father.

He had come home early from his office.
"What's going on here?" he asked Uncle Jack as he entered the room.

"Sarah refused to listen to me from the moment she got home from school today," Uncle Jack lied. "I'm warning you, Matt, this little lady is going to give you nothing but problems!"

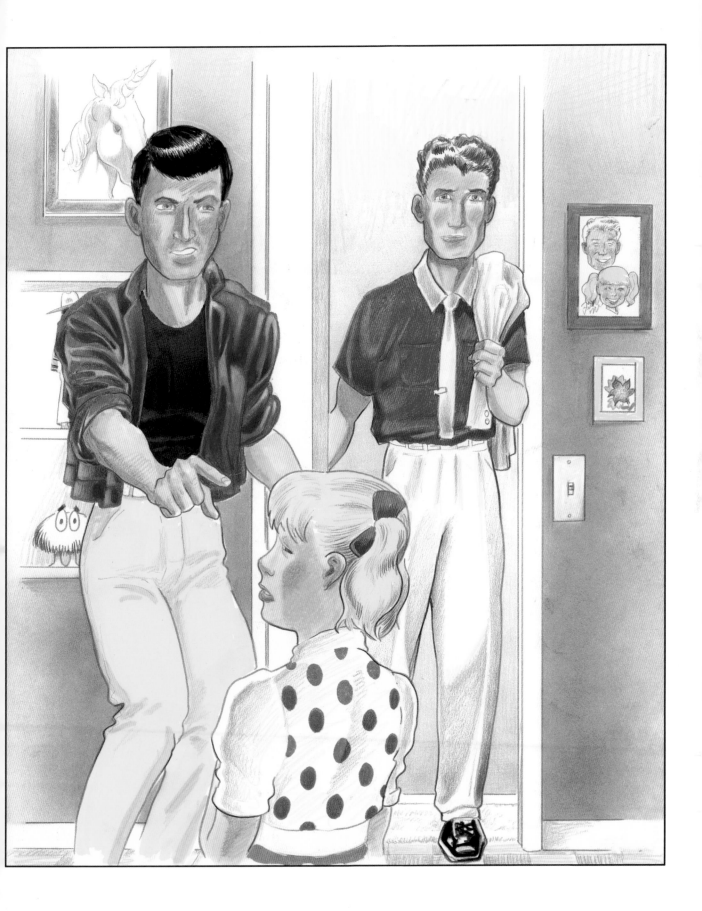

Sarah's father turned to her. "Apologize to Uncle Jack immediately," he ordered, not even asking her what she had done.

Sarah did not know what to say.
She had done nothing wrong.

What had happened?
Sarah used to have fun with Uncle Jack.
He used to take her to the park and to the movies.
Why wasn't he nice anymore?
She was not bad. She tried her best to always be good.

Sarah felt ashamed. She felt confused.
What could she say?
She stared at the floor.
Her words would not come out of her mouth.
They were stuck.

"You'll stay in this room until Uncle Jack gets an apology, young lady," said her father as he left the room with her uncle.

It seemed like forever as Sarah stood there.
Her heart was pounding inside her chest.
She did not move. She couldn't.
Soon her gentle heart beat softly once again.
After awhile, Sarah heard nothing at all.
There was only silence.
It was as if something had popped inside of her,
like she had separated from the rest of the world.
Sarah felt like her feet were glued to the floor;
and as the sunlight left her room,
Sarah found herself standing in darkness.

The grandfather clock struck six as the door opened downstairs. "Sarah, Matt, Jack, I'm home," Sarah's mother called out as she entered the house.

Maybe Sarah heard people talking softly downstairs, maybe not. But it all seemed so far away.

Sarah's sadness was drifting away.
She had no feelings at all, but was like a stone statue.

A moment later her mother knocked on her door.
"Sarah," she said, "May I come in?"

Sarah did not respond. She couldn't.

Her mother entered her room and turned on the light.
There stood Sarah! She did not move. She did not speak.
"What happened, sweetheart?" asked her mother gently.

Sarah did not respond. She couldn't.

Her mother hugged her, kissed her, patted her head, shook her.
But Sarah remained like a stone statue, unable to move,
unable to speak.

"Matt!" called Sarah's mother loudly. "Call Doctor Good on the phone. Tell him we are bringing Sarah right over. Something is terribly wrong."

"What could have happened to our Sarah, Matt?" asked Sarah's mother as she carried her downstairs.

"I don't know, dear," replied Sarah's father. "When I came home from the office my brother Jack was in her room. He told me she had given him trouble from the moment she got home from school."

Sarah's father looked worried as he started the engine.

"Have you noticed that Sarah has not been acting right lately?" her mother asked.

"Yes! Now that you ask, I have noticed a change in her," replied her father. "Sarah has so many friends, but she has not been playing with them."

"I can't even get her to go horseback riding, Matt. You know how she loves horses," said her mother, who was now more puzzled than ever.

Doctor Good and Nurse Wendy were waiting for them as Sarah's father carried her into his office.

"What has happened to Sarah?" asked Doctor Good.
"Has she been sick?"

"No," replied Sarah's mother.
"But we have seen changes in her behavior.
 Sarah has not been eating well.
 She has been having a problem going to the bathroom.
 She has not been sleeping very well; and
 she spends a lot of time alone in her room reading books."

"She doesn't seem to be playing with her friends,"
her father added. "Come to think of it, I have not seen
Sarah smile for some time. I have been so busy at my office
that I hadn't thought about it until this very moment."

Doctor Good scratched his head.
He wondered what had happened.
This was a mystery.

Nurse Wendy looked at Sarah closely. She wondered what had happened. "Sarah," she finally asked, "Do you hear me?"

Sarah did not respond. She couldn't.

"Sarah," Nurse Wendy asked again, "Will you look at me? Can you speak to me? Can you tell me what is wrong?"

Sarah did not respond. She couldn't.

"We are all worried about you, Sarah," said Doctor Good.
"I am going to examine you.
We need to find out what is wrong."

"Please go into the waiting room," he said to her parents.
"Nurse Wendy will help me."

Doctor Good checked Sarah's ears and throat. He listened to her heart and pushed on her tummy. Everything seemed fine.

Then Doctor Good remembered what Sarah's mother had said about Sarah's problem going to the bathroom. He checked her bottom.

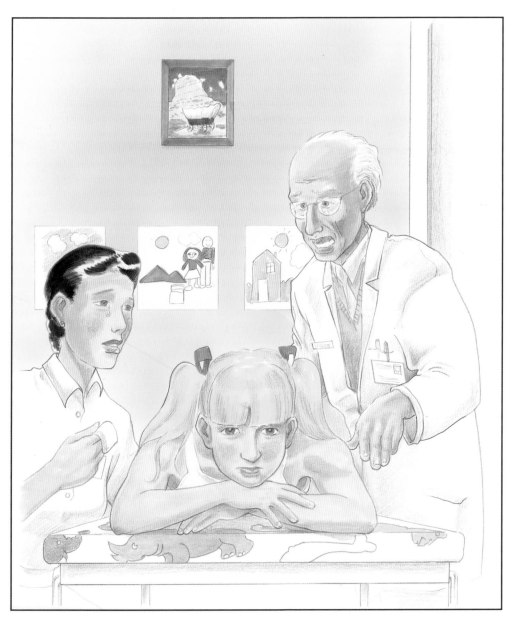

"Oh, no!" he said sadly.
"Oh, Sarah! Someone has hurt you."

Doctor Good looked at Nurse Wendy. She was crying.
The doctor had tears in his eyes, too.

Doctor Good took Sarah's face in his hands and looked into her eyes.

"Everything is going to be all right," he said.
"You can speak to me, Sarah. I will listen to you.
I will believe you. I will protect you."

Sarah began to sob. A flood of tears streamed down her lovely face.

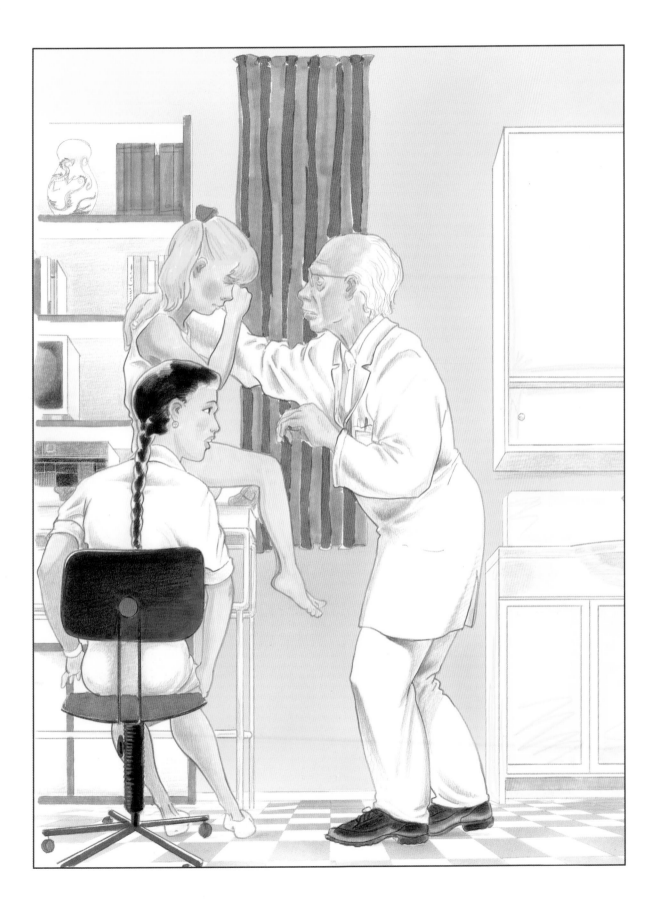

"There, there," said the doctor as he held her tenderly.
"It's all right. You're safe now.
Please tell me who hurt you."

"I can't tell you," she said.
"He said nobody would believe me."

"Who told you? Who are you talking about?" Doctor
Good asked again. "Please tell me. I am your friend.
I will help you."

Sarah could not hold back the truth any longer.
"It's Uncle Jack," she cried. "My uncle tells lies.
Sometimes he scares me. Sometimes he hurts me.
He said if I told anyone, he would hurt my mother.
Please don't let him hurt my mother."

"Uncle Jack is not going to hurt your mother, and Uncle Jack
will never hurt you again either," promised the doctor.

"Nurse Wendy will stay with you while I speak to your mother and father," said Doctor Good as he left the room. "I'll be back in a few minutes."

Nurse Wendy squeezed Sarah's hand.
She had known Sarah since Sarah was a tiny baby.
Sarah was one of Nurse Wendy's favorite patients.

Doctor Good sat down at his desk.
"Sit down, please," he said to Sarah's mother and father.
"You must listen to every word I say."

The doctor told them all he had learned. They were very upset.
They were very angry at Uncle Jack. Uncle Jack had done
something very bad, something grownups should never do.
He had hurt a child.

"There is no excuse for what Uncle Jack has done,"
said the doctor. "I am telephoning a special place called
Child Protective Services. I need to tell them what has
happened. Child Protective Services protects children.
They will help you and they will help Sarah."

"Our children do not make this happen," continued
  the doctor.
"They are innocent. They need to feel safe.
  They need to know they can trust grownups.
  They need to know we will believe them.
  They need to know we will protect them."

"Uncle Jack has committed a serious crime.
  He cannot be with Sarah.
  He cannot be in your home.
  Other children must be protected from him too."

"Education is the key to change," said Doctor Good.
"Our schools can help.
  They can teach children the difference between
  good touching and bad touching.
  They can help them grow up feeling good
  about themselves."

"What about Sarah?" asked her mother.
"Is she going to be all right?"

"With the right kind of help she will get better,"
  replied the doctor.
"Speak to her. Tell her how much you believe in her.
  Tell her how much you love her."

"I will telephone my friend, Doctor Fine.
  She is a special kind of doctor that helps children share
  their feelings. She can help Sarah.
  In fact, we will all help Sarah," said Doctor Good.

"May we see Sarah now?" asked her mother.

"Of course," responded Doctor Good, as he
  led them out of his office.

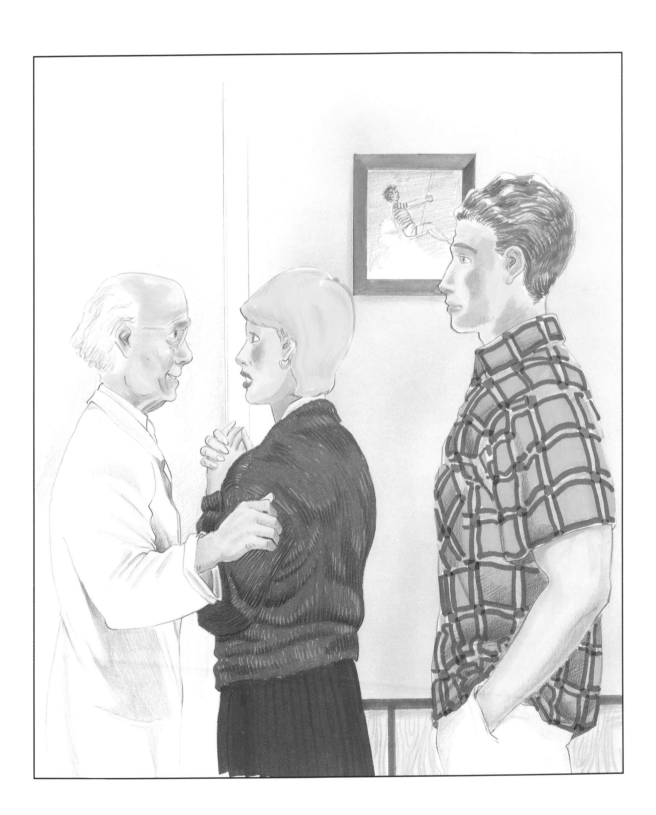

Sarah looked up at them sadly.

"Oh, my little Sarah," said her father.
"We love you more than anything else in the whole world.
 What Uncle Jack did was wrong.
 He will never hurt you again.
 Your mother and I are here. We will always be here."

Sarah felt so tired. It had been such a long day.

Things were going to get better she thought,
as her father lifted her into his arms.
Her mother and father understood. Now, she would be safe.

Epilogue

Sexual assault upon children today, and in the past, is now being recognized as one of the major, long-standing factors in childhood and adult psychopathology. The concept of 'trust' inherent in the parent-child relationship has long been accepted as a basis for positive emotional growth and personality development from infancy to adulthood. Yet today there are multiple studies indicating that one in three adult women and one in four adult men have been victims of some form of sexual assault prior to the age of 18 years. Tragically, 75–85 percent of such cases have been committed by a person well known to the child and family. It will be someone who intentionally and without conscience violates the 'basic trust' inherent in all adult-child relationships of responsibility. It will be a family member, relative, or other adult already known to the child and family.

Ironically, however, much of the primary prevention and early education given to our children only alerts them to possible dangers from a stranger. Is this because we are still uninformed about the 'intra-familial' risks toward children, or is it that parents and society are in 'denial'?

Sarah is a remarkable story of a child living within a supposedly risk-free family, a child who was repeatedly and without conscience violated and abused by a trusted family member. This poignant, insightfully written story reveals many psychologically important elements necessary for preventing and recognizing this problem. It is the tragic childhood of Sarah and the inspirational message of the author which bring to conscious awareness the awesome incidence of this ongoing trauma of children. The abuse of trust and victimization of a minor by adults who purposely and with awareness use power, authority, intimidation and a professing of love to commit these atrocities must be confronted head-on by society.

Sarah, written in a language understood by young children, does just that. It reveals behavioral signs which should alert every mother and father to the possibility of earlier victimization. It stimulates its readers to a heightened sense of alertness with respect to the recognition and identification of high-risk family/social/interpersonal relationships. Prevention through education is paramount in importance. When this fails, a child is at risk. *Sarah* clearly presents not only the tragic consequences of such failure in prevention, it also presents an optimistic and essential understanding of the multi-disciplinary approach to rehabilitation of both the victimized child and the emotionally devastated parents.

The reporting requirements, the liaison between law enforcement, social services, the courts and the judicial system are all a part of the rehabilitation process and the psychotherapeutic recovery. It is through such a multi-system approach that the risks of victimization can be reduced and hopefully eliminated. Where such preventive intervention fails, society must be prepared to respond immediately in terms of well-funded programs and highly-trained, available specialists in this area.

Sarah will go a long way towards facilitating awareness and education of children, parents and society. It will also enhance the 'coming-out' and rehabilitation-recovery process of thousands of adult men and women who themselves in their own childhood were violated and assaulted by the brutal use of misused authority of 'trusted adults.'

Sarah and its author, Illana Katz, are to be highly commended for putting into words a tragic aspect of childhood and family life. These words, now shared with the community of families, will hopefully stimulate further research and rehabilitation study of childhood sexual victimization. Once recognized, society must then vigorously pursue the remediation of a family tragedy, which although only recently recognized has been the plague of generations of children and adults.

Morris J. Paulson, Ph.D.
Professor of Psychiatry
Department of Psychiatry and
Biobehavioral Sciences
University of California
at Los Angeles